Dedicated to my flock of lifetime friends
Judy, Teddy, Ann Marie, Penelope, and the 2 Terrys.

DM

To my most precious grandchildren, whom I love to infinity.

SJB

™

Text copyright © 2013 by S. J. Bushue
Illustrations copyright © 2014 by Deb McQueen

Special thanks to Marlee Coyne, Robin & Blake Hicks, George Hunt, and Alex & Jennifer Smith

All inquiries should be addressed to:
The Little Fig, LLC™
P.O. Box 26073, Overland Park, KS 66225 USA
www.thelittlefig.com
Printed in USA
So Big & Little Bit Adventures™ are trademarks of The Little Fig, LLC™

First Edition, September 2014
Library of Congress Control Number: 2014912514

ISBN-13 978-1-63333-004-7

So Big & Little Bit Adventures™
Creators S. J. Bushue & Deb McQueen

Cattle roam in herds,

El ganado vaga en rebaños,

but not a covey of quail.

pero no un grupo de perdices.

Cranes stroll in herds,

Las grúas dan una vuelta en rebaños,

Deer gather in herds,

Los ciervos se reúnen en manadas,

but not a prickle of porcupines.

pero no una punzada de puercoespines.

Dinosaurs grazed in herds,

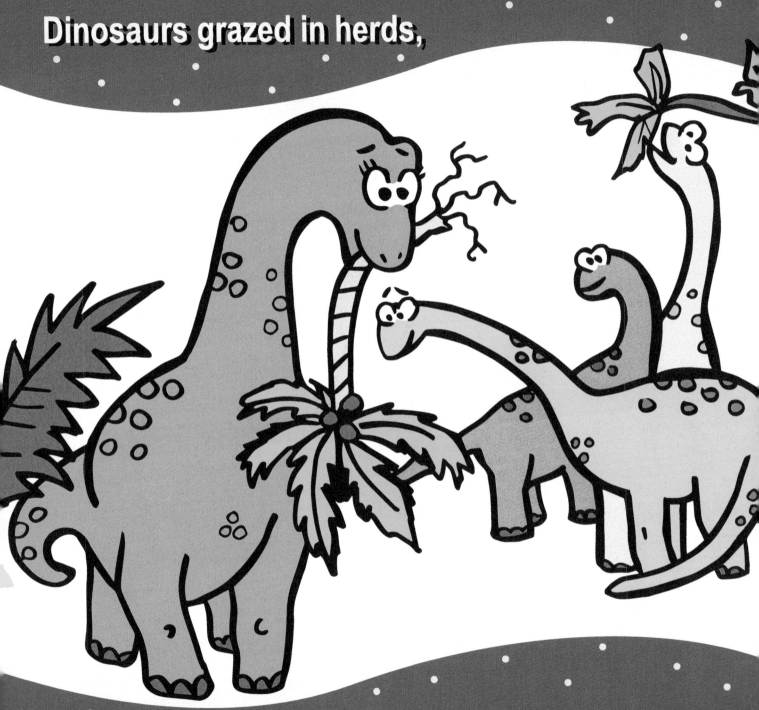

Los dinosaurios pastaban en manadas,

but not a flamboyance
of flamingos.

pero no una extravagancia de flamencos.

Elephants tromp in herds,

Los elefantes marchan en manadas,

but not a horde of hamsters.

pero no una horda de hamsters.

Hippos play in herds,

Los hipopótamos juegan en manadas,

but not a flutter
of butterflies.

pero no un aleteo de las mariposas.

Kangaroos hop in herds,

Los canguros saltan en manadas,

but not a pride of lions.

pero no una manada de leones.

Llamas trail in herds,

Las llamas arrastran en rebaños,

but not a knot of toads.

pero no un nudo de los sapos.

Moose munch in herds,

Los alces mascan en manadas,

but not a business of ferrets.

pero no un negocios de los hurones.

Pigs party in herds,

Los cerdos andan de fiesta en manadas,

Reindeer prance in herds,

Los renos cabriolan en manadas,

but not a watch of nightingales.

pero no un reloj de ruiseñores.

Seals chill in herds,

Las focas se relajan en manadas,

but not a pod of dolphins.

pero no un grupo de delfines.

Walruses feed in herds,

Las morsas se alimentan en manadas,

but not a rookery
of penguins.

pero no una colonia de pingüinos.

Yaks graze in herds,

Los yaks pastan en manadas,

but not a charm of hummingbirds.

pero no un encanto de colibríes.

Zebras gallop in herds,

Las cebras galopan en manadas,

but not a troop
of monkeys.

pero no una tropa de monos.

Animals in order of appearance.

Cattle roam in herds, but not a covey of quail.

Cranes stroll in herds, but not a tower of giraffes.

Deer gather in herds, but not a prickle of porcupines.

Dinosaurs grazed in herds, but not a flamboyance of flamingos.

Elephants tromp in herds, but not a horde of hamsters.

Hippos play in herds, but not a congregation of alligators.

Horses run in herds, but not a flutter of butterflies.

Kangaroos hop in herds, but not a pride of lions.

Llamas trail in herds, but not a knot of toads.

Moose munch in herds, but not a business of ferrets.

Pigs party in herds, but not a gaggle of geese.

Reindeer prance in herds, but not a watch of nightingales.

Seals chill in herds, but not a pod of dolphins.

Walruses feed in herds, but not a rookery of penguins.

Yaks graze in herds, but not a charm of hummingbirds.

Zebras gallop in herds, but not a troop of monkeys.

CPSIA information can be obtained
at www.ICGtesting.com
Printed in the USA
BVOW07*0806250916

463227BV00012B/45/P